Published by Advance Publishers, L.C.
Maitland, FL 32751 USA
www.advancepublishers.com
Produced by Judy O Productions, Inc.
Designed by SunDried Penguin

Tarzan
Printed in the United States of America

First published 2003.

Deep in the African jungle, Kala the gorilla rescued a human baby from the claws of Sabor the leopard. She decided to be his mother and she named him Tarzan.

The chief gorilla, Kerchak, wasn't happy about allowing this strange child into their family.

As Tarzan grew up, he learned the ways of the jungle but knew he'd always be different from his gorilla family. And Kerchak still didn't accept him.

Over the years, Tarzan grew strong. He learned to swing through the vines and spring up the trees. He learned gorilla language and even developed his own special Tarzan yell.

One day, Tarzan came across a girl!
She was being chased by some baboons
and Tarzan swung to her rescue.
Her name was Jane and she'd come
to Africa with her father and the
hunter Clayton to study gorillas.

Tarzan was delighted but bewildered to discover that Jane was just like him – a human.

Kala knew it was time to tell Tarzan about his real parents. She took him to the tree house where she'd found him and Tarzan realized he really belonged in Jane's world. He told Kala he was going away with Jane, but said, "You will always be my mother."

When Tarzan had said his goodbyes to his jungle family, he boarded the ship with Jane. But Clayton's men tied him up and told him of their plan to capture the gorillas. Tarzan let out a cry, and his friends heard his call and swam out to help him.

Tarzan and his friends raced back to the jungle, followed by Clayton and his men. Clayton aimed his gun at Tarzan, but Kerchak charged him and was shot instead.

As Kerchak lay dying, he asked Tarzan to forgive him and to always look after his gorilla family.

Tarzan knew that his place was in the jungle and he sadly let Jane get back in the boat.

But Jane knew her place was with Tarzan so she leapt off the boat and rushed into his arms.

The End